THE DYNO—MITE DOG SHOW

THE SECRET KNOCK CLUB

THE
DYNO–MITE
DOG SHOW

BY **Louise Bonnett-Rampersaud**

PICTURES BY **Adam McHeffey**

SCHOLASTIC INC.

ISBN 978-0-545-69249-6

Text copyright © 2012 by Louise Bonnett-Rampersaud.
Illustrations copyright © 2012 by Amazon Content Services LLC. All rights reserved.
Published by Scholastic Inc., 557 Broadway, New York, NY 10012, by arrangement with Amazon Children's Publishing. SCHOLASTIC and associated logos are trademarks and/or registered trademarks of Scholastic Inc.

12 11 10 9 8 7 6 5 4 3 2 1   14 15 16 17 18 19/0

Printed in the U.S.A.   40

First Scholastic printing, January 2014

Book design by Anahid Hamparian
Editor: Margery Cuyler

To the original Agnes Mary Murphy (O'Toole)
1917–2009
Rathvilly, County Carlow, Ireland

Contents

Chapter 1

Mrs. Duncan took off her glasses. When they're not on her face, her glasses hang from her neck on a string.

They look like they're bungee jumping.

Mrs. Duncan always takes off her glasses for important announcements.

So we can see her "pay-attention-here" eyes better.

And this time I *was* paying attention.

Because my name was in the important announcement.

And not for the regular stuff, like "Agnes, please pick your coat up off the floor," which she says even though she tells us to make ourselves at home.

This time, the important announcement was about our community service project.

"Class," Mrs. Duncan said. "This is your last chance. Does anyone want to join Agnes and her team for their community service project? As you know, when I first asked you to form teams, I didn't realize that the members of The Secret Knock Club would insist on staying together," she said, pointing to me. "But now that they have, their team should really be open to anybody else who wants to join it."

She looked around the room.

So did I.

To make sure Heather Kellogg wasn't raising her hand to be an "anyone."

I looked up the aisle. Heather always sits in the front row, right in front of the teacher. She's a teacher's pet.

Only, unfortunately, no cage.

Heather had a pink ribbon in her hair and was wearing pink pants and a pink T-shirt.

She looked like a giant carton of strawberry milk. A carton I didn't want spilling over into our project!

This is what we were doing: a dog show at the old folks' home. They were going to wear costumes and bark songs and everything!

The dogs.

Not the old folks.

We brain-hurricaned up our ideas in class last week. Brain-hurricaning is just like brainstorming, only better. It's a top-of-the-line brainstorm!

This is what our team came up with:

#1 COINS FOR THE CRITTERS. HELP YOUR LOCAL ANIMAL SHELTER!
#2 RE-SIGH-CLING. IT'S NOT AS BORING AS YOU THINK!

Learn how to mash your trash and other great tricks!

And . . .

#3 WRITING TO THE WRINKLED (my mother said this sounded disrespectful, so we changed it

We couldn't decide on just one, so we finally came up with planning a dog show for the old folks' home this coming Saturday at 2 o'clock.

Only now I was worried that Heather might join in, and all because of Mrs. Duncan and her "no-team-should-be-exclusive" announcement.

I raised my hand.

"Yes, Agnes?" Mrs. Duncan asked.

I used my "pay-attention-here" throat, which means I cleared it really loud. "It's very kind of you to be thinking of us and all, but we really don't need any extra people to help with our team project," I said. I leaned in closer. "After all, I have had some experience with organizing projects, you know."

Which was true.

Last year, I organized a campaign to educate students about the importance of eating a well-rounded breakfast.

Only Principal Joy made me take down my posters because she said eating a well-rounded breakfast didn't mean eating only round things, like doughnuts.

I gave her a new name after that.

Principal Not-Such-A-Joy.

Even the lunch lady had agreed with her, although I said that maybe, since she was a *lunch* lady, perhaps she wasn't an expert on *breakfast* foods.

well-rounded breakfast

"Agnes," Mrs. Duncan said, shaking her head. "We've already gone over this. It's a school rule that you can't do a community service project at school as a *club* unless you open it up to others in the class who might want to participate." She shrugged. "That's just the rule, I'm afraid."

"Well?" she asked again. "Anyone?" she said, putting her glasses back on the end of her nose, like her nostrils needed to see the class or something.

And that's when it happened.

That's when the pink milk carton raised her hand.

And Heather Kellogg was joining our team for the project!

Chapter 2

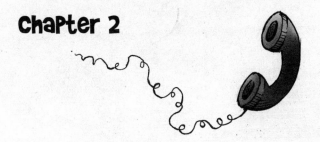

I CALLED HEATHER AT 8 O'CLOCK ON THE DOT the next morning.

Because of Mrs. Duncan.

Plus, I always call people on the dot!

This time I'd chosen a green one. Our kitchen floor is covered with green and tan dots, so I always stand on one when I make calls.

Especially official club business calls.

There are five of us in The Secret Knock Club.

Actually, make that six, since Heather is a sort of only-in-the-club-until-the-community-service-project-is-over member.

Our clubhouse is in my backyard.

We have a lot of snacks.

And, of course, we each have a secret

knock to get in. That's why we're The Secret
Knock Club.

I cleared my throat before I spoke to get
rid of any frogs or tadpoles that might be in
there.

"I am calling from The Secret Knock

Club," I said in an English accent. "May I please speak with a Miss Heather C. Kellogg of 42 Woodbury Way?"

I always use an English accent for club business, because it makes me sound more official.

It does *not*, as Fudgy, a member of the club says, make me sound like I have a stuffy nose.

"Agnes?" Heather said. "Is that you?"

"Yes," I said. "This *is* Miss Agnes Murphy of The Secret Knock Club. I am delighted to speak with you."

"Agnes?" Heather asked again. "Are you okay? What's wrong with your voice?"

"I am fine, Miss Heather C. Kellogg of 42 Woodbury Way. I greatly appreciate your concern. Now, the reason for my call this morning is to remind you that the next meeting of The Secret Knock Club to discuss community service projects and other issues will be today, after school, at three thirty p.m. on the lawns of the Murphy residence."

"You mean your backyard?" Heather

asked. I could tell she was probably rolling her eyes.

I took a deep breath.

"Precisely," I replied.

Heather laughed. "Precisely?" she asked. "Did you just say 'precisely,' Agnes?"

"Just be there at three thirty and don't be late!" I shouted and hung up the phone.

Being English is not as easy as it seems!

I was putting finishing touches on the meeting agenda when Skipper showed up. Skipper's always chewing gum and blowing the most amazing bubbles. We play a game with them. It's just like the game where you guess what shape a cloud is.

Only his bubbles don't stay puffy for as long.

blowfish bubble

His real-alive name *is* Skipper, even though everyone thinks it's a nickname.

"What's all that?" Skipper asked, trying to get a peek at the agenda. He looked puzzled.

I stepped in front of the board.

"Nothing," I said, trying to cover it up. "You'll find out later. Ummm . . ." I said, looking around the fort. "Can you find the binoculars?"

This is called changing the subject.

I am almost a professional at it.

"Binoculars?" Skipper asked. "What for?"

"You'll see," I said. "Can you just find them?"

I looked around the fort.

It's my most favorite place in the world to be.

Once you get in, that is.

First, you have to give your secret knock. Then, you have to climb through the door that's in the floor. Sometimes, if you get stuck pushing yourself up, you feel like a jack-in-the-box. I tried to get my dad to move the door to the roof last year, but he thought there would be too many accidents that way.

Once you get in, there's a Visitor's Center, which is really just a bowl of candy.

Fudgy hangs out there a lot.

And on the walls, we have tons of pictures.

We also have a place for our knock-knock joke of the week.

Knock, knock.

Who's there?

Howie.

Howie, who?

Howie gonna get rid of Heather?

I was admiring my work when I saw her walking across my yard. I quickly crossed out the "get rid of" part and wrote "welcome" (even though I didn't mean it).

"Skipper!" I called. "The binoculars?"

He handed them to me.

Heather always looks like a flower girl. This time she was wearing a big white dress with black patent leather shoes.

She had a huge bow on the top of her Curly-Q-Fry hair.

She looked like a present.

The kind you'd want to return.

Emma was walking behind her.

Emma's not at all fluffy. Which is good. Because I am not fond of fluffy outsides on people other than grandmothers. And possibly small babies.

I ran across the yard to meet them.

I looked around for something to use.

"Here," I said, grabbing the scarf off Heather's neck. "Cover your eyes. You need to be blindfolded."

"What for?" she asked, pushing the scarf away from her face.

"So you don't see where the fort is."

She scrunched up her eyes. "But it's right there!" she said, pointing across the yard. "I know I haven't been here since last year, but it's not like it's moved or anything."

I ignored her.

"Can you grab me those, too?" I asked Emma, pointing to some acorns on the ground. "We need to plug her ears so she can't hear our secret knocks."

"Agnes!" Heather yelled, trying to pull away from me. "Have you gone crazy?"

"Nope, not crazy!" I said, trying to think of something fast. "It's just part of our new . . . security plan, that's all. We've had a couple of break-ins lately."

Which was *sort of* true. Fudgy *had* come back a couple of times at night to grab some candy from the Visitor's Center.

We walked her to the ladder and up into the fort.

"Can you take this stuff off me now?" Heather said from behind the scarf. Her voice was kind of muffled because I had sort of, accidentally, covered some of her mouth, too.

"Yep," I said. "Let's start the meeting."

"But The Cape's not here yet," Skipper said.

The Cape's real-alive name is Evan, but we all call him "The Cape" because back in kindergarten he made a Super-Hero cape and wore it every day. Only he spelled it with two *p*'s, so he was a Supper-Hero.

A defender of dinner.

He still wears that cape sometimes. Only now he's crossed out one of the *p*'s.

"He'll be here in a minute with Fudgy," I said. "Let's start."

Skipper and I sat down on his beanbag.

Emma stood next to Heather in the back.

I made a note in my head to talk to Emma about that later. When I make a note in my head, I use a pretend pencil because I don't want any pretend ink sticking to the insides of my brain.

Skipper looked up. He had a puzzled look on his face. "That's what you were writing earlier?" he said, pointing to the agenda. "But we don't do *that*." He laughed.

I looked at the list.

"We don't do what?"

"*That!*" he said, pointing again.

"Yes, we do!" I said quickly.

"No, we don't!"

Fudgy shook his head, too.

"We do *not*, Agnes! We do not *knit* in The Secret Knock Club."

24

"Well . . . we do *now*," I said. "This is the kind of stuff the new, improved Secret Knock Club is all about. It's all part of our, umm . . . doing community service projects and stuff like that." I turned to Heather. "Of course, if any of this sounds like it's too boring for you or something, you're welcome to join another team for the project."

Fudgy swallowed a chocolate chip cookie whole. "Since when do we 'COME UP WITH WAYS TO HELP THOSE WHO NEED HELP WITH STUFF?" he yelled, reading down the list. "ALWAYS, ALWAYS ALWAYS THINK OF OTHERS FIRST?" he said, laughing. "Where did you come up with this stuff? What happened to making spitball sculptures and having pie-eating contests like we normally do?"

Everyone started laughing.

Except for me.

I started glaring.

At Heather.

I wanted her to leave before we went inside my house to make dog biscuits for the dog show.

But she didn't leave.

So I did!

I climbed down the ladder and ran ahead of everyone into my house.

Chapter 3

I PUT RAT-A-TAT ON MY HEAD.

Rat-A-Tat is my thinking cat. Other people have thinking *caps*, but I have a thinking cat.

"Where's Mom?" I asked Grandma Bling. "Is she still at yogurt class?"

"It's *yoga*, Agnes," she said. "And yes, she is. She'll be back any minute to help make the dog biscuits. We didn't think you'd be done with your meeting so fast."

"Neither did I," I said.

Grandma Bling is my mom's mom. She

lives with us now on account of Grandpa Hoover having a very bad case of being dead, although Grandma Bling says that's not a very nice way of saying it.

Grandma Bling is not her real-alive name. We call her that because she's got lots of sparkle and dazzle. She's like a Christmas tree full of ornaments that somebody forgot to take down.

Except she doesn't have a star on the top of her head. Unless you count her tiara. But she only wears that on BINGO night and when we play Room Service.

She handed me a plate of peanut butter-and-jellyfish sandwiches.

Peanut butter-and-jellyfish sandwiches are my favorite snack in the whole world.

What you do is put peanut butter, jelly, and red Swedish fish on a piece of bread and chomp away.

I took a small bite. "Where's everyone else?" Grandma Bling asked. "Aren't they coming in to make the biscuits?"

I looked out the window. The Cape had finally shown up. Heather was leading the way in her big white dress. The club looked like a wedding party.

"Here comes the bride now," I said.

Grandma Bling pulled out the recipe card. PEANUT BUTTER POPPY POPPERS it said at the top. PERFECT FOR YOUR POOCH!

I grabbed the card. "Might as well get this over with," I said under my breath.

Heather opened the back door. She walked in and waved to Grandma Bling.

"Hi, kids," Grandma Bling said. "Come on in."

Fudgy walked over and looked at the recipe. "Peanut butter!" he said. "My favorite."

"They're for dogs," I said, taking the card back. "Sit, Fudgy, sit!"

He grabbed a peanut butter-and-jellyfish sandwich and sat down.

Fudgy loves food. That's why he's the

CEO of The Secret Knock Club. Chief *Eating* Officer.

We all took a seat around the table.

"Since The Cape's here now, I guess we can start," I said.

I handed out the papers.

"I want to go over these before we make the biscuits," I said.

I'd made a list of everyone's responsibilities for the project.

They all read down the list.

I looked up just in time to see Heather's eyes get really, really big.

And not in a good way.

Chapter 4

"Poop?" Heather yelled, reading down the list. "I'm in charge of poop?"

"Yep," I said. "The Cape's in charge of posters. Skipper's in charge of props. Fudgy's in charge of snacks . . . making them, not eating them. Emma's in charge of decorations. And you're in charge of—"

"Poop!" she screamed again.

"Yep. Poop," I answered. "We're going to have the best dog show ever. And the great part is you get to wear this."

I threw her the T-shirt I'd made. She held it up and read what I'd written on the front.

"'I'm the Poo in Pooch'???" she screamed. "Agnes!!!"

She used a tone kind of like when my

parents call me by my "lots-of-syllables" name. It's always *Agnes Mary Murphy, why does your hair have green stripes in it?* Or, *Agnes Mary Murphy, why is Rat-A-Tat hanging from the light like that?*

"What?" I answered. "Is it the wrong size?"

Just then my mom walked in the door. It seemed like the calmness from her yogurt class had been zapped right out of her.

"What's going on here, girls?" she said. "Is something wrong?"

"Nothing's wrong," I said, hoping Heather wouldn't hold up her shirt. "I just gave Heather her shirt for our community service project, that's all." I leaned in close to my mom. "I think it might be the wrong size or something," I whispered.

"Oh, I see," my mom said. She looked over at Heather. "Don't worry if it doesn't fit, sweetie. You'll definitely have a shirt to wear for Saturday. I'm sure Agnes will see to that, won't you?" she said, smiling at me. "And I bet once you try it on, it will all be fine, anyway."

Heather glared at me.

"Now then," my mom said, looking around the table. "How are the biscuits coming along?"

Fudgy spoke up. "We haven't even started making them yet." He grabbed another sandwich and shoved it into his mouth.

"I see," my mom answered. "Just give me a minute to change and I'll come right back to help." She gave Grandma Bling a we've-got-our-hands-full-here, don't-we? face, as she walked up the stairs.

Grandma Bling made rearview mirror eyes at me. Rearview mirror eyes are the look she gives me in the car when I need to be more polite.

Only this time, she was making them without a car.

I thought fast.

"I'm going to wear a shirt, too, you know," I said to Heather. "We all are, right guys?"

Everyone nodded.

"Oh, *really*?" Heather said, looking at me. "What are *you* in charge of?"

"Ummm," I said.

Grandma Bling was staring at me, waiting for the more polite part.

"Well, it's hard to say, *exactly.* . . ."

"What do you mean?" she asked.

"I'm in charge of a little bit of everything, I guess. . . ."

"Oh, *yeah?* Let me see *your* shirt."

I slowly reached under the table to find it.

"Let me see it," she said again.

I lifted it up.

And there, in big letters, was my shirt.

Heather read the words out loud: "TOP DOG!"

Then she stood up really fast. Which is not a good thing to do when you're in a big dress and close to a table.

There was a loud sound that was not a good sound.

"My dress!" she cried, which was also not a good sound. There was a huge rip in the front of it. She threw her hands up in the air and knocked something off the shelf.

"I want to go home!" Heather screamed. "Can somebody just take me home?"

My mom came running down the stairs.

"What's going on?" she asked. "Is everyone okay?" She saw Heather. "Agnes," she said, turning to me. "Why is Heather covered in flour?" She grabbed a dish towel and tried to dust her off.

Grandma Bling held up the car keys. "Agnes and I were just about to take Heather home, weren't we, honey?" she said, nodding for me to follow her. "I think she's probably had enough for one day."

I peeked over at Heather.

She looked like a ghost.

A very mad ghost who definitely had had enough for one day.

I glanced at her dress. The ripped part looked like a handle hanging down. Like maybe if I turned her upside down, I could carry her.

Only I didn't think it was a good time to offer.

So instead we hopped in the back of Grandma Bling's car. Grandma Bling has a "talking" car, which is what I call it because it doesn't have a TV or anything else fun, so the only thing to do is talk.

Although this time there wasn't much talking.

Except for when I told Heather I knew the shirt would fit.

Chapter 5

worm poop

"ROOM SERVICE!" GRANDMA CALLED OUT.

I wrote LIFE IS A MR. E. (which is my mystery-like way of writing the word mystery) in my journal.

I've had a journal since kindergarten. It's called DISCOVERIES, by Agnes Murphy. Now I'm on volume 2. It's called EVEN MORE DISCOVERIES, also by Agnes Murphy.

"Room Service!" she called out again.

Room Service is a game Grandma Bling and I play when we need cheering up. Sometimes, when she needs it, I put on an apron and knock on *her* door, and many times, when *I* need it, she does the same for me.

I opened the door a crack. Grandma was wearing an apron, a tiara, large lipstickied lips, and slippers. She was carrying a plateful of cookies and two glasses of milk.

"Cookies for Room 209," she said with a wink.

Even though our house has four bedrooms, she and I painted the number 209 on my door, because we think it sounds more "hotelish" with bigger numbers.

She walked in and sat on the edge of my four-poster bed. "Just what I ordered," I said, taking a cookie off the plate.

Show-off Heather Kellogg has a four-poster bed with a huge canopy over it in her room.

I know from when we used to be friends.

So I made a four-poster bed for my room, too. This is what I did: I took four posters (two of very famous singing people and two

of sharks) and taped them to my bed. I even added a canopy, too. Or in my case, a "Can-o-Peas."

Grandma took Rat-A-Tat off my head.

"Let's do the chips," she said, taking me in her arms.

The chips is our nickname for the real dance of the salsa.

Grandma likes to dance her way through problems. Sometimes it's the waltz. Sometimes it's the rumba.

She says it tickles her fancy to dance.

And Grandma's got a lot of fancy to tickle.

"Doing this project is going to be good for you, Agnes," she said, her hips going around and around like a washing machine. "It's always good to learn to get along with others."

And here's the thing.

I *do* get along with others.

As long as it's someone *other* than Heather Kellogg.

I did my no-breath talking, which is talking really fast without stopping for punctuation, eating, or peeing.

"How can you say that, Grandma? How can you even think I could get along with her? Don't you remember what she did to me? There's no way I am *ever* going to get along with a traitor like that. NEVER. NEVER. NEVER."

My DISCOVERIES journal is full of things. Things I discover. Like how worms go to the bathroom. And things I like to keep secret.

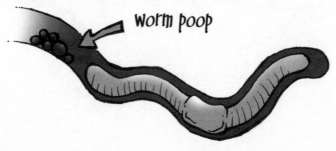

worm poop

Only last year, Heather found my journal when she came for a sleepover. Then she read it and blurted out my most important, Top Secret secret of second grade to the whole entire bus on a field trip. She said I had a crush on Alex-not-Andrew.

And the thing is, I don't even like Alex-not-Andrew anymore.

Alex-not-Andrew is a twin.

He's Alex.

Not Andrew.

So that's what he calls himself: "Alex-not-Andrew."

Andrew   Alex-not-Andrew

Grandma sat down on my bed. "I think I'm getting too old for the Chips," she said, rubbing her back. "But I'm not getting too old for some good advice, young lady. Come over here," she said, patting the bed.

I finished my cookie and sat down beside her.

She looked me in the eye. "Look, Agnes," she said. "I'm not saying what Heather did was right. She really hurt your feelings. And I'm sorry for that. But we all make mistakes, right? And hasn't she tried to apologize over and over again? Maybe it's time you gave her some slack, huh?"

"Gave her some slacks?"

"No," she said, chuckling. "Some slack. You know, lighten up a little." She paused for a second. "Think of it this way," she said. "You just need to try to be nice to Heather for this one project, and then, when it's over, nobody's saying you have to be best friends again or anything. Although I think you might be surprised. . . ."

I thought about it for a minute.

"Oh!" I said. "You mean like a No-Thank-You Friend?"

In our house, when there's food we don't want to eat, we have to take a "No-Thank-You" bite. This is how it works: We take a bite of the slimy or gooey or green stuff that we don't want to eat, and if we really don't like it after that, we can say, "No Thank You, I Don't Want Any" and we don't have to eat anymore.

So, that's what Heather was now. A "No-Thank-You Friend." All I had to do was work with her on this one project and when it was done, I could say: "No thank you, I don't want to be your friend anymore."

I gave Grandma a hug.

'Cause that's what you do to grandmas who give you advice.

And homemade cookies.

And then I imagined my "No-Thank-You Friend" as a big pile of spinach that I would never have to eat again.

Because even though I didn't say it, I

thought Grandma Bling was wrong about Heather and me.

Either way, I'd find out soon enough.

The dog show was only a few days away.

Chapter 6

On the bus the next morning, I pulled out my towel.

My "Agnes-does-not-sit-on-bus-seats" towel.

Bus seats are all crinkly and rippled. Like alligator skin. You never know if there might be a tooth or something stuck in there.

And that's not even the worst part.

To me, the bus is like a great big shark. It pulls up and opens its great big mouth and sucks all the kids into its belly.

Then it spits them back out at the end of the ride.

Fudgy sat down next to me. He has lots of freckles on his face, so we always play a game with them. It's like connect-the-dots, only with freckles. Last week I thought I found a dinosaur, but it turned out the tail was just some pancake syrup from his breakfast. When he wiped it off, the whole thing was ruined.

It was like watching extinction.

"Here," I said, reaching into my backpack. "Take one."

I gave some pieces of paper to Emma, Fudgy, Skipper, and The Cape, too. I even gave one to my No-Thank-You Friend. On the front were the words *Middle Secret*.

There are three levels of secrets in The Secret Knock Club. Top Secret. Middle Secret. And Low Secret.

My Middle Secret message read: *Meeting of The Secret Knock Club. Go over dog tricks. Today. Upper playground. During recess.*

Heather popped her head over the seat, like a nosy neighbor.

"We're doing dog tricks at recess today?" she said, very loud.

I put some huffy eyes on her.

"You're not supposed to say it out loud, Heather," I said. "That's why it's a SECRET."

Heather Kellogg is NOT! NOT! NOT! an expert at secrets.

I took a deep breath, staring at my No-Thank-You Friend.

"Just be there," I said, as the bus pulled up to our school, Lakeview Elementary.

The door opened and spit us all out.

Right in front of Principal Not-Such-A-Joy.

Principal Not-Such-A-Joy always greets the students in the morning. Like "Hello, Agnes, no, you cannot bring your cat to school tomorrow," and things like that.

She had her hair done in her principal bun. It was pulled back really tight, like it wasn't allowed to come out and have any fun.

I tried to lighten things up. "Good morning, Principal," I said. "Exceptional Community Service Volunteers coming through."

We gave her a high-five and walked into the school. We went down the main hall to the gym. In the mornings, the gym is where we wait before we go to our classes. During the day, the gym is where we have PE, or as I call it, PU, because everyone stinks so much when they're done.

Especially the boys.

Mrs. Duncan came and took us to class. We looked like a line of turtles walking down the hall with our backpacks on.

After morning announcements, Principal Not-Such-A-Joy poked her head into the classroom.

"Good morning, everyone," she said. She had on a happy face. "Just curious to see how your community service projects are coming along. Last years' were so great, I'm looking forward to seeing what you kids have come up with this time."

Mrs. Duncan looked up from her desk. She put down her pen.

"Oh, come in, Mrs. Joy," she said, standing up. "The kids have some wonderful things planned for this year." She turned and looked at us. "In fact, I'm sure they'd love to share some of their ideas with you, wouldn't you, class?"

Which is what teachers always say when the principal is in the room.

Samantha and Matthew went first. They were going to hold a bake sale to raise money for some new books for the library. Ellen, Katie, Alex-not-Andrew, and Annie were having a hula-hoop-a-thon to raise money for the animal shelter. Paige Smithers and Amanda Kong were going to play the flute and the trumpet for the elderly. They were calling it "FLUTE" and "TOOT."

Principal Not-Such-A-Joy nodded.

"Well, it sure sounds like you've got some great projects this year, Mrs. Duncan. Please let me know if there's anything I can do to help."

She headed for the door.

"We're doing a dog show!" I blurted out.

She turned around.

"Sorry?" she asked, turning back. "Did you say something, Agnes?"

Principal Not-Such-A-Joy always remembers my name without me having to tell her. She says there are some students you can never forget.

Plus, I'm a frequent visitor to her office.

"Yes, Principal Not . . . I mean . . . Principal Joy. We're doing a dog show. This Saturday at two p.m. at the Brookside Retirement Village."

"Really?" she said, clapping her hands excitedly. "What a coincidence. That's where my mother lives!" She looked thrilled with the news. She walked back to my desk.

Her eyes lit up. "I have a great idea, Agnes. I'm free on Saturday. Why don't I come, too!

In fact . . . you could put Trudy in the show. She'd love it!"

Trudy is Principal Not-Such-A-Joy's dog. Not her mom.

Her dog is part beagle. Part mutt.

TRUDY

It's a butt!

I didn't know how to answer her.

But it didn't matter, 'cause she kept right on going. "So, it's settled then. Saturday it is. See you there," she said.

And she left the room.

There should be a rule about principals being allowed to have butts!

Chapter 7

"WHY'D YOU DO THAT?" FUDGY AND SKIPPER asked at recess.

Skipper was holding up the hula hoop for Heather to jump through since he's our prop guy.

"Do what?" I said.

We were practicing dog tricks.

Only, no dogs.

Just Heather jumping through the hoop.

And, okay, maybe barking, too.

"Tell Principal Not-Such-A-Joy about the dog show!" Fudgy said.

"Yeah," Skipper added.

"Now she's coming. And

bringing her dog! Don't you remember what she did last year at the Spring Fair?"

Of course I remembered!

She went to the bathroom in the dunk tank.

Trudy.

Not Principal Not-Such-A-Joy.

We called it the "stunk tank" after that.

I was about to remind them that Heather was on poop patrol this year, but she started talking first.

"Agnes didn't mean to, you guys," she said. "She was just excited about the project." She turned to look at me. "Right, Agnes?"

Which is *not* what I thought she was going to say!

And then a strange thing happened.

I agreed with my No-Thank-You Friend.

I took a deep breath and mouthed "thank you" at her.

Which is *not* what I thought I would do.

Although it wasn't like a *real* thank you or anything, 'cause of the no voice and all.

Just then Ellen, Katie, Alex-not-Andrew,

and Annie came over.

"Hey, that's *our* hula hoop," Alex-not-Andrew said. "We need it back to practice for our hula-hoop-a-thon."

That boy had better manners when I liked him!

I got huffy.

"Is not," I said, taking it from Skipper.

"We've been using it to practice every day," he said. "Give it back." He grabbed the other side of the hoop.

I was very glad that boy was NOT my boyfriend.

I switched to my English accent. It was now official Secret Knock business.

"We are also practicing, young Alex-not-Andrew," I said, slowly and Englishly. "Would you kindly take your hands off our hoop?"

"Practicing for what?" he said. "You're doing a dog show. There aren't any dogs here. What do you need a hula hoop for? And anyway, what's up with your voice?"

"Dear, dear, young Alex-not-Andrew," I

said. "For the dog *tricks*, of course. We are jumping through the hoop to see what the dogs should do at our community service event this Saturday afternoon."

"Then what's with those?" he said, pointing to the ground. "What kind of tricks are you doing with those?"

I looked down. I tried to kick the brownies away before Fudgy got too close to see.

"Ummm . . . those are for practicing proper scooping techniques," I said in a very soft, Englishy accent.

But it was too late.

"My brownies!" Fudgy yelled. "Are you kidding me, Agnes? I *knew* I had some in my lunch!"

He gave me a frowny brownie face.

But before Fudgy or Skipper could get

really mad, the playground lady came to see what was going on.

Alex-not-Andrew pulled on the hula hoop again.

It flew out of our hands and up into the air.

And here's the thing.

Playground ladies do *not* look good with hula hoops around their necks.

Chapter 8

COMMUNITY SERVICE PROJECTS ARE DANGEROUS.

I tried to explain that to Principal Not-Such-A-Joy after I was sent to her office for lassoing the playground lady.

"I think we should cancel the community service projects, Principal Joy," I said. "Things are getting too dangerous."

I looked out on the playground. I was pretty sure Heather was limping. Principal Joy raised her eyebrows high like she was trying to see if they looked better on the top of her head. It's what she does to make room for her eyes to get bigger when they're shocked.

"Cancel them, huh?" she said from behind her desk.

Principals always sit behind big desks. Probably to protect themselves from the kids.

"Yep," I said. "For the safety of the children." I looked out the window again. "And the playground ladies," I added.

Principal Not-Such-A-Joy put her eyebrows back in place.

"Tell me, Agnes, whose idea was it to have the children jumping through hula hoops on the playground in the first place?"

I stared at her PRINCIPAL-YOU'VE-GOT-A-PAL-IN-ME sign.

Even though I didn't think she was being very pally just then.

"And whose idea was it to spread *these* all over the playground?" she asked, pulling a bunch of brownies out of her pockets. She put them on the edge of her desk.

I acted like I did not recognize those brownies.

"Perhaps if we just think these things through a little more," she said, "the world of community service projects won't be quite so dangerous." She stood up and wiped off her pants. "Or chocolaty," she said.

She bent over to scratch her ankle.

"Now . . . there was something else I wanted to mention to you about Saturday, since it doesn't look like we'll be canceling it after all," she said, picking up some papers with her other hand. "If I could just find . . ." She flipped through the papers.

Then she sat down to scratch her ankle again.

Then her arm.

Then her leg.

Then her ankle again.

She looked like she was doing an itchy dance.

"What on earth?" she said, still scratching her leg. "I'm itching everywhere!"

And that's when I saw it.

Okay, *them*.

Crawling along the edge of her desk.

By the brownies.

I reached forward and scooped up the brownies.

And the ants.

This is called getting rid of the evidence.

"Well, Principal Joy," I said, backing up to the door. "Thank you very much for your advice." I held up the brownies. "Too bad about your itching. But I hope you feel better soon. I'll just throw these in the trash on my way out." I pointed to the brownies. "Wouldn't want to leave crumbs all over the place."

"Fine, fine," she said, without even looking up from scratching her ankles. "I'll talk to you later, Agnes."

Which is what I was afraid of.

Because it turned out I was right.

Community service projects *are* dangerous.

Especially when your principal has ants in her pants.

Or at least very near her pants.

Chapter 9

"ANTS?" GRANDMA BLING ASKED.

"Ants," I said. I pointed to the diagram. "Pretty much all over, I'd say, by the way she was scratching." I'd drawn a picture of Principal Not-Such-A-Joy to be helpful. There were arrows pointing to the itchy parts. With brown marker hairy dots for the ants.

Grandma Bling's eyes said "I see" all by themselves. Her mouth didn't have to say a thing!

She reached into the sock to make sure there wasn't another note. One that said bees or snakes or locusts or something.

Grandma Bling and I have a "Sock-It-To-Me" program. This is how it works: We put notes inside socks when we want to send each other a message and then hang them on our doorknobs. It's just like e-mail. Only smellier.

She put the note down and cupped my face in her hands.

"Do I even want to know how?" she asked.

"I don't think so," I said, shaking my head. "Let's just call it a bad batch of baked goods."

"I see," her mouth finally said.

But it didn't get to say anything else, because just then the doorbell rang.

Heather was standing on the front porch.

Miss Heather C. Kellogg of 42 Woodbury Way.

She was holding a basket of something, like Little Red Riding Hood.

I spoke in my official, club-business English accent.

I figured that was the only reason she was knocking at my door.

And I was right!

"My mom and I made the dog biscuits for the show on Saturday," she said, handing me the basket. "We figured you might have been out of flour." She paused. "There should be enough for all the dogs, I think."

"How *mah*velous of you, Heather!" I answered, still using my accent. I pulled back the cloth to get a peak. "That was very, very thoughtful." I had to admit, Peanut Butter Puppy Poppers smelled pretty good. For people who aren't even dogs. "Now, I'm sure, with such a long journey ahead, you'll want to be on your way back to your mother's house. Good day, Miss Heather Kellogg."

I started to close the door.

But Grandma Bling made her rearview mirror eyes at me.

She does that a lot when Heather's around.

Then she bent down and whispered something in my ear.

"It's an English accent," I whispered back.

Grandma Bling's eyes rolled around like searchlights.

Grandmas are experts with their eyes.

"On second thought," I said, "want to come in?"

Heather's eyes lit up.

She followed me into the kitchen.

"So . . ." I said, putting the basket on the counter.

"So . . ." Heather replied.

"So . . ." I said again, "what do you want to do?"

I gave up on the English accent. Being English is very tiring.

Heather shrugged. "I don't know, what do you want to do?"

I shrugged back at her.

It was like our shoulders were talking to each other.

Which was just fine with me.

Because maybe that way our mouths wouldn't have to.

"I have an idea," Grandma Bling said. "Why don't you both go up to Agnes's room, and I'll whip up a little snack for you guys." She winked at me. "I'll give you a shout when it's ready."

I went up the stairs first.

I didn't want Heather-eyes on my journal.

The last time she was in my room was when she'd read my DISCOVERIES journal and found out I liked Alex-not-Andrew.

I wanted to make sure Heather-eyes didn't discover EVEN MORE DISCOVERIES this time.

But then I remembered.

My journal was hidden under my mattress.

Heather looked around my room.

"Wow," she said. "It looks different in here." She pointed to my posters. "Those are cool."

My face turned pink. Which is what it does when I get embarrassed and don't want somebody to know I put them up to have a four-poster bed like theirs.

"Thanks," my pink, embarrassed mouth said.

We sat down on the edge of my bed.

"Agnes?" Heather said.

"Yeah?"

"I have to tell you something." She looked

up at the ceiling, like maybe she'd written some notes up there to help her. "I had a crush on him, too," she said.

"Huh?"

"You know. Last year. Alex-not-Andrew. I had a crush on him, too."

"You what?"

"That's why I told everybody on the bus that you liked him. I wanted him to be so embarrassed that he wouldn't like you back. 'Cause you're more . . . well . . . you know . . . like-ier." She got off my bed and started pacing around my room.

"Like-ier?"

"Yeah, you know, people like you more than me. And I didn't want him to like you. I wanted him to like me. But he didn't. And I'm sorry."

I couldn't believe it.

All this time, I thought show-off Heather Kellogg was just mean.

But she wasn't.

Well, okay, a little.

But there was an even better part.

She was jealous, too.

Jealous of me!

"Apology accepted!" I said.

I flew down the stairs on happy feet when Grandma Bling called us.

Having a jealous friend makes you do that.

"Mmmm . . . what did you make?" I asked, smelling the goodness in the air.

"Your favorite," Grandma Bling said, pulling the pan out of the oven. "Brownies!"

I looked over at Heather.

And, guess what?

We laughed out loud together.

And, okay, maybe we smiled at each other, too.

Chapter 10

LATER ON WE HAD A CLUB MEETING TO GO OVER
the checklist for the show.

And guess what?

No blindfolds this time!

Only here's the bad thing. Emma couldn't
come. She was sick. "Sick as a dog," her mom
said, when she called to tell us.

Which I thought, under the circumstances,
wasn't the nicest way to say it.

But there was an even more bad thing.

Emma's mom wasn't too sure Emma
would be better by Saturday!

I broke the news to the rest of the club.

"The show's on Saturday, guys," I said,
"and Emma's really sick. Her mom doesn't
know if she'll be able to make it by then."
I ran my finger down the list. "Let's see

what else we have to do to get ready. I guess someone needs to take over the decorations for her."

Heather raised her hand. "I'll do them," she said.

I wrote "jealous friend" next to "decorations."

"And Fudgy," I said, looking up again. "Do you have the snacks together?"

"Huh?" he asked, putting a gobstopper in his mouth.

"The snacks. For Saturday. Do you have them yet?"

He stopped chewing for a second. "Yeah, I guess. I'll probably just bring some cookies and a bag of chips or something."

"*One* bag of chips?" I looked at him kind of funny. "I was thinking more like five."

"Five?" Fudgy asked, his mouth still trying to crack the gobstopper. He looked confused. "Okay. But I don't think I'm gonna be able to eat that many. My mom's making pancakes that morning, so I probably won't be too hungry."

Every Saturday morning, Fudgy's mom makes a Pancake Slam-o-Rama. He calls it that because if he doesn't get enough

pancakes, he slams his hands down on the table for more.

I felt like slamming my hands down, too. "Fudgy, when I asked you to bring snacks for the show, I meant for everybody else. Not just YOU."

I wrote down "GET MORE SNACKS" on my list.

I stood up in front of everyone.

"Okay, listen up, everyone. Order in the fort! Order in the fort!"

That's what judges say to get people's attention. Only they use a big hammer kind of thing instead of a branch with a tin can tied to the end.

Fudgy's eyes lit up. "I'd like a ham and cheese!" he yelled from his beanbag.

I rolled my eyes at him. "Fudgy," I said, kind of huffy. "'Order in the fort' means to be quiet, *not* what you want to order to eat."

Fudgy got real quiet.

And he didn't get a ham and cheese.

I turned to The Cape.

"Okay, how about you? How are the posters coming?"

"Great," he said. "Everything's under control."

Just then my mom knocked on the door.

"Honey," she said, poking her head up through the floor. "Principal Joy just called. She said she had something she was just itching to tell you, and she didn't want it to wait until tomorrow."

Itching to tell me?

I pictured my diagram in my head.

But then I smiled and acted like my principal calls me at home for things all the time.

"It's about Saturday," she said, squeezing the rest of the way through the door.

Oh, good, I thought.

"Turns out they're not allowing outside dogs to the event," my mom said. "It's a bit of a risk. You know . . . you wouldn't want a dog biting one of the residents or anything. But the good news is you *are* allowed to use the employees' dogs, as long as the employees are with them. So, last count, you're up to ten dogs in the show. Isn't that exciting? That's more than you thought you'd have."

She clapped her hands happily. Like a seal.

And let me tell you. That *was* exciting news.

Principal Joy's butt couldn't be in the show!

"Well, 'bye then, kids," my mom said. "Good luck with the rest of the planning. I know it's going to be great." She started to climb down the ladder. But halfway down she remembered something. She slapped her hand on her forehead. "Oh, I almost forgot to tell you the best part!" she said. "Principal Joy pulled some strings over at the home, and they said she could still bring her dog. Because of her mom and everything."

And before you know it, the butt was back!

Chapter 11

THE SECRET KNOCK CLUB MET AGAIN A FEW more times and all of our plans were in place.

It was finally Saturday, Community Service Project Day!

After lunch, I hopped into Grandma Bling's talking car and honked the horn.

"Come on, Grandma! Come on, Mom!" I called out. "The dogs are waiting." Dad couldn't make it to the show. He was out of town for work. But he had called earlier from the golf course to say good luck.

Grandma Bling put on her sunglasses and got into the car.

Mom got into the front with her.

I looked at Grandma Bling in the rearview mirror.

She looked like a giant bug.
"Step on it," I yelled from the backseat.
We were like a getaway car.

And guess what?
No rearview mirror eyes this time.
'Cause of the giant sunglasses.
We pulled up in front of the Brookside Retirement Village.

I saw one of our posters on the front door. I smiled.

"Drop me off here, please, Grandma," I said, all excited. "I need to see that poster."

I ran up to the front door and read the poster: COME AND SEE OUR PEST!

PEST??? And The Cape said the posters were under control? Leave it to a "Supper-Hero" to write PEST and not PETS!

Things were NOT off to a good start.

I opened the door hard and went inside.

Fudgy was sitting on the couch in the lobby.

"Come on," I said, grabbing him. "We've got a pest problem to take care of."

"Huh?"

"You'll see," I said, pulling him along. "Where's The Cape?"

"I don't know. Putting up more posters, I think."

"Well, come on. We've got to stop him."

We ran down the hallway. A woman with a clipboard was coming toward us. "Excuse us. Excuse us. Pest control. Coming through!" I yelled.

She stopped in front of us and tapped her clipboard. "Excuse me, young lady," she said. "What on earth are you talking about?

"There are no pests in this facility. No mice or rodents of any kind!" She looked up and down the hallway. "It's the cleanest place you'll ever find. Now, if you would please lower your voice. You'll scare the rodents . . . I mean, the residents!"

I saw The Cape by the back door. "Don't mean to be rude, ma'am, but you do have a pest problem." I pointed down the hall. "And there it is now." I grabbed Fudgy again and kept running. "Sorry, gotta go!" I yelled to the clipboard lady.

We ran over to the door.

"Here," I said to The Cape, handing him

a marker. I pointed to the poster and read aloud: "'COME AND SEE OUR PEST'???"

I looked at him like he was one.

The Cape laughed. "Oh," he said, changing around the S and the T. "There. Better?"

I read it again. COME AND SEE OUR PETS.

"Much," I said. "Let's go change the rest of them."

We headed for the lobby. A little woman with marshmallow-colored hair was sitting in a wheelchair by the front door. She had lines going up and down all over her face.

She looked as if she was quilted.

"Here for the dog show?" she asked.

I smiled at her quiltedness. "Yep," I said. "Just as soon as we get rid of all the pests in this place." I fixed the spelling on another poster. "Shouldn't be long now."

Her mouth made a big O for "Oh my!" and she wheeled herself over to the clipboard woman.

Fudgy, The Cape, and I went outside to change the last poster.

We were almost done when Grandma Bling, Mom, and Principal Not-Such-A-Joy showed up. Grandma Bling was carrying the dog biscuits.

Mom was carrying some of our supplies.

And Principal Not-Such-A-Joy was carrying her butt.

"Where would you like these?" Grandma Bling asked.

I looked up. "Inside, Grandma," I said. "There's a big room on the left where the dog show's taking place. You can't miss it. Thanks."

"And where would you like Trudy?" Principal Not-Such-A-Joy asked. She was wearing a jogging outfit, sneakers, and her hair was not in a bun.

She looked different.

Not so principally.

"Oh," I said, handing the marker back to The Cape. "Well, the other dogs aren't ready yet. So if you just want to hold on to her . . ."

Principal Not Such-A-Joy looked down at Trudy. She gave her a smile. "Of course I'd love to hold on to you, wouldn't I, my little Trudy Wudy?"

Trudy Wudy?

What was going on with Principal Not-Such-A-Joy?

We walked inside the lobby. Principal Not-Such-A-Joy went over and started talking to someone. Then she turned to me and waved. "Yoo-hoo, Agnes. Would you come over here, please? I'd like you to meet someone." She pointed to a woman. "Agnes, this is Meredith. Meredith Hanson. She's in charge of Brookside. If you have any questions, don't hesitate to ask her. "

She gave the woman a hug.

Ms. Hanson looked over her glasses. "I believe we've already met," she said, reaching out to shake my hand.

My face turned red. I put my hand out to shake hers, too.

"I like your clipboard," I said.

"And this," Principal Not-Such-A-Joy said, pointing to the woman in a wheelchair, "is my mom, Mrs. Eleanor Joy."

Principal Not-Such-A-Joy bent down and gave her a hug. Trudy wagged her tail and licked her quiltedness.

And her marshmallow-colored hair!

Chapter 12

"LISTEN UP. LISTEN UP, EVERYONE," MEREDITH "Clipboard" Hanson said a little while later. "We've only got an hour till showtime!" She checked her watch. "Better get a move on."

I looked around the room.

We still had a lot to do!

I never thought I would say it, but I couldn't wait for Heather to get here. She was probably running late because of the extra decorations she was bringing from her birthday party last year.

She had a DOGGONE FUN! party.

Or at least the decorations had said so.

But I wasn't there. So I doubt it was *that* DOGGONE FUN!

Skipper walked in with all the props.

"Over here," I said, pointing to the end of the runway. The employees had built a runway in the middle of the room for the dogs to walk up and down.

But I was adding a little "Agnes" touch.

I'd made a sign that said POOCH PARADE.

Skipper walked past the POOCH PARADE runway and put the props down. He had a hula hoop. A whistle. A tambourine. A harmonica. And music.

"Looks great," I said. "Now, let's decorate the bridal suite."

The "Bride and Groom Suite" was where we were going to "groom" the dogs before the show.

It was really just the janitor's closet.

At the end of the show, it was where two lucky dogs were going to get dressed for their wedding.

That's right!

One lucky dog couple was going to get married.

The Cape and I put balloons and streamers near the bridal suite, and up and down the POOCH PARADE runway.

Fudgy set up the snacks. He put a sign above them: DOGGONE HUNGRY.

Heather finally walked in.

With her I'M THE POO IN POOCH shirt on.

And a big white medical mask over her face.

She looked like a doctor.

"For the smell," she said. "And the possible dog allergies."

And then I remembered something about Heather from when we were friends before. The always-thinking-something-was-wrong-with-her part.

Some things never change!

I grabbed a bunch of the decorations and

helped her put them up.

When we were done, the place looked DOGGONE FUN great.

The employees and their dogs were lined up and ready to go. We brushed the first dog in the bridal suite closet and made an announcement. "Showtime!" I called out.

The residents started coming in and lined up next to the POOCH PARADE runway.

Some were in wheelchairs.

Some were in little carts they had driven into the room.

And others were in chairs.

I nodded to Skipper.

He pressed "play" and started the music.

The residents began clapping.

The first dog and her owner walked down the runway. The dog was a poodle named Sprite. Her owner was Betty, one of the nurses at Brookside. They both had tight curly hair, like little white brussels sprouts. Sprite was wearing a pink sweater with red hearts all over it. There were "Oooh's" and "Aaah's" from the residents.

Then came Scrapper. He was an English

bulldog with a floppy face. His owner was Frankie, a cook at Brookside. Frankie had a floppy face, too. Like a stack of pancakes.

Skipper stood at the end of the runway

with his harmonica. And Scrapper howl-howl-howled!!! along to the music.

When he was done howling, Scrapper and Frankie high-fived each other.

And I am not kidding about that!

Then there was Lulu, the Chihuahua. Her owner, Veronica, wheeled her down the runway in a suitcase. Lulu was a purse dog so she wasn't used to walking too far. She barked at all the balloons as she rode by.

After Lulu, the other dogs came down the runway with their owners. One stopped and licked somebody's hand. One barked to the tune of "Happy Birthday." A few showed off their outfits. And some jumped through hoops.

Okay . . . hoop.
And then it was Trudy's turn.
We dimmed the lights for extra effect.

Chapter 13

PRINCIPAL NOT-SUCH-A-JOY PUT TRUDY ON HER leash. It was a pink one with rhinestones on it. She stood at one end of the runway and waited for her cue.

Skipper stood at the other end of the runway and held up a hula hoop.

I nodded for Principal Not-Such-A-Joy to start.

They took two steps down the runway and Trudy stopped.

She wouldn't budge.

Principal Not-Such-A-Joy tugged on her leash.

Skipper called out. "Here, Trudy, here!" he said.

But Trudy just stood there.

And she did not move.

Skipper put the hula hoop down. "Okay," he said. "How about this?" He started howling to the music.

But Trudy just stood there.

And she did not howl.

Principal Not-Such-A-Joy's mom wheeled herself over to me. I bent down for her to whisper something in my ear.

I looked up at Heather.

Mrs. Eleanor Joy was right!

I ran over to Heather.

"Take it off," I whispered.

She started lifting up her T-shirt.

"What are you doing?" I said, pulling her shirt back down. "Not your *shirt*. Your *mask*. It's scaring Trudy. She probably thinks you're a monster or something!"

Heather yanked off the mask.

And Trudy wagged her tail.

Then she ran down the runway and jumped through the hoop.

I mouthed "thank you" to Mrs. Eleanor Joy.

She winked back.

"Clipboard" Hanson was standing by the door.

She looked pleased, too.

I continued. "And now," I said, "for what you've all been waiting for. The names of the two lucky dogs for the wedding ceremony."

I pulled a name out of the boys' hat and announced it.

And then I pulled a name out of the girls' hat.

There was a shriek from the audience when I announced the name.

Principal Not-Such-A-Joy started jumping up and down.

Then she started screaming: "I'm going to be the mother-of-the-bride!"

Chapter 14

"THE MOTHER-OF-THE-BRIDE! I'M GOING TO BE the mother-of-the-bride!" Principal Not-Such-A-Joy was still saying minutes later. "Agnes," she said, handing me Trudy, "could you please hold her for a minute? There's so much to do before the wedding!" She looked at herself in a mirror. "My hair!" she said, trying to poof it up. "I must do something with this hair," she muttered to herself as she walked out to the lobby.

I took Trudy to the Bride and Groom Suite.

"One bride coming up," I said, putting her down on the table.

I reached in a bag and pulled out the wedding skirt my mom had gotten for us at the thrift shop.

Heather and I put the skirt on Trudy.

After the veil, which was really just a napkin from the cafeteria, we were ready for the wedding.

Principal Not-Such-A-Joy came back in the room and sat down next to her mother. She had flowers in her hair. They looked a lot like the flowers from the desk in the lobby.

She was glowing.

Principal Not-Such-A-Joy asked if I could walk Trudy up the aisle (which was really just the runway). She said she was feeling too emotional to do it.

I agreed.

Then I nodded to Frankie.

He started walking with Scrapper.

Only no howl-howl-howling!!! this time.

'Cause Scrapper was the groom, that's why!

He was wearing a doggie tuxedo. His bow tie was in the shape of a bone.

When he reached the end, I nodded for Skipper to start playing "Here Comes the Bride."

Everyone turned to watch Trudy.

Only that's when a bad thing happened.

I put Trudy down for a minute to find her leash, and, POOF, she was gone.

I had a case of a runaway bride!

I didn't know what to do.

I grabbed a pen and held up a sign for Heather to see. It was one of the DOGGONE FUN! ones from the decorations.

Only I'd crossed out the word *fun*.

Chapter 15

THE AUDIENCE WAS GETTING RESTLESS.

Principal Not-Such-A-Joy kept looking up from the edge of her chair.

Heather came running over.

"I can't believe it. I've lost the butt!" I said.

"Clipboard" Hanson overheard me.

"You've lost the *what*?"

I looked up at her.

Principal Not-Such-A-Joy was checking her hair in a little compact mirror.

"Clipboard" Hanson was my only chance!

"I mean my principal's butt," I told her. "I've lost my principal's butt."

She was speechless.

And possibly a little faint.

"Follow me," I said.

We walked into the Bride and Groom Suite closet.

I pulled out a picture from my pocket.

"Have you seen this dog?" I asked her.

She took the picture out of my hand. "That's Trudy, the bride," she said, "your principal's dog. Is Trudy missing?"

I nodded.

"I see," she said.

"Yes, but have you seen *her*?"

The closet door opened.

It was Principal Not-Such-A-Joy!

Ms. Hanson quickly hid the picture.

"What on earth is going on?" Principal-Not-Such-A-Joy asked. She looked over our shoulders. "Where's Trudy?"

"Now, now, Mrs. Joy," Ms. Hanson said. "You wouldn't want to ruin the surprise, would you? Let's just say that Agnes and I have something up our sleeve. Now, if you'll just go back to your seat we can get started."

"A surprise?" Principal Not-Such-A-Joy asked. "For my Trudy Wudy?"

"Trust me. It will be a surprise for everyone!" Ms. Hanson said. "Now, run along," she said, shooing Principal Not-Such-A-Joy back to her seat.

She turned to me. "Come on," she said, putting down her clipboard. "No one knows this place better than me. We'll find her, don't worry."

I signaled to Skipper to change the music and then asked Heather a huge favor.

"Show them some pooper scooper techniques or something," I said, pointing to the audience. "Anything to distract them."

I handed her the Pooper Scooper 2000, which was really my mom's old salad tongs, and followed Ms. Hanson to look for Trudy.

We called for Trudy up and down the halls of the residents' bedrooms. We even checked in Mrs. Eleanor Joy's bedroom to see if she was hiding there.

But no luck!

Then Ms. Hanson had another idea.

We dashed to the kitchen.

And that's when we saw it.

Something white sticking out the door.

Something white that was in a huge case of ice cream!

"Oh dear!" Ms. Hanson said, chuckling. "It looks like somebody forgot to put this vanilla ice cream back in the freezer."

Just then we heard Principal Not-Such-A-Joy's voice. "Trudy? Agnes?" she called from the hall. "Are you almost finished with the surprise?"

Ms. Hanson tiptoed over and closed the door.

She picked Trudy up, pulling her away from the ice cream, and tried to wipe her down.

"Yep. She's finished. I mean, *we're* finished

with the surprise," Ms. Hanson said from inside the kitchen. "Everything's fine. We'll be right there." She giggled a bit. "I think she had a little case of cold feet, as well," she said, smiling at me. She wiped Trudy's paws again. "But she's definitely over that now."

We waited for Principal Not-Such-A-Joy's reply.

"Wonderful!" she said from the other side of the door. "What a relief. I'll see you back in the room, then."

We changed Trudy's veil and walked back to the show.

I gave Skipper the "pinkies-up" sign to start the music again. "Pinkies-up" is the

same thing as "thumbs-up."
It's just that the
thumbs must get
tired of being used so
much, so I give the
pinkies a turn sometimes.

Heather stopped her
demonstration on proper
scooping techniques and jumped
down from the runway.

We dimmed the lights.

And I walked Trudy carefully down the aisle.

When we reached Scrapper, he spent the

whole time licking the paws of his bride.

Vanilla was obviously his favorite flavor!

"Oh, look," Principal Not-Such-A-Joy said out loud. "It really is true love!"

She put her hands over her heart and smiled a "happy-mother-of-the-bride" smile.

I looked over at Ms. Hanson.

She smiled, too.

An "it's-our-little-secret" smile.

But then her mouth stopped smiling.

And she pointed to the runway.

To the poop!

I looked at Heather.

She grabbed a bag and ran up to the

runway before anyone else saw it.

But I stopped her.

I took the bag out of her hand and walked over to the poop.

And, I, Agnes Mary Murphy, scooped the poop.

'Cause that's what you do for jealous friends who help you with a community service event.

And it worked. Principal Not-Such-A-Joy never even saw it. She was too busy picking up a cookie. "Let's celebrate," she said, before taking a bite. "To the bride and groom and a successful community service project."

I looked at the cookie.

My eyes got big.

Heather leaned over and whispered to me. "Don't worry, Peanut Butter Puppy Poppers are okay for humans, too," she said.

And we laughed out loud together.

And okay, we smiled at each other, too.

Louise Bonnett-Rampersaud lives with her husband and two children in Sandy Spring, Maryland.

The author of several picture books, including *Never Ask a Bear* and *How Do You Sleep?*, she's working on the next adventures of **THE SECRET KNOCK CLUB**. Stay tuned for Books # 3 and 4!

Adam McHeffey is the illustrator-author of *Asiago*, a picture book about a small vampire who has a challenging day at the beach.

Also a professional musician, Adam lives in Brooklyn, New York.